COULD YOU SURVIVE
THE CRETACEOUS PERIOD?

BY ERIC BRAUN
ILLUSTRATED BY ALESSANDRO VALDRIGHI

Content Consultant: Mathew Wedel, PhD
Associate Professor, Department of Anatomy
Western University of Health Sciences
Pomona, California

CAPSTONE PRESS
a capstone imprint

You Choose Books are published by Capstone Press, an imprint of Capstone.
1710 Roe Crest Drive
North Mankato, Minnesota 56003
www.capstonepub.com

**Library of Congress Cataloging-in-Publication Data is available on the Library
of Congress website.**
ISBN 978-1-5435-7401-2 (library binding)
ISBN 978-1-4966-5807-4 (paperback)
ISBN 978-1-5435-7406-7 (eBook PDF)

Summary: Leads readers through a Cretaceous Period adventure in which they can
choose what to do and where to go next.

Design Elements
Capstone and Shutterstock: DianaFinch, Miceking, Studio Photo MH

Editorial Credits
Editor: Mandy Robbins; Designer: Bobbie Nyutten; Media Researcher: Jo Miller;
Production Specialist: Tori Abraham

All internet sites appearing in back matter were available and accurate when this
book was sent to press.

Printed and bound in the USA.
PA100

TABLE OF CONTENTS

TRAPPED IN THE PAST

YOU are an ordinary kid going about your everyday life. Suddenly, you find yourself in a strange place and a strange time. It's a period from long ago. The world looks different than anything you've ever seen before. Terrifying beasts roam the land. Danger lurks at every turn. Where will you find shelter? How will you get food? Will you ever see your friends and family again? Most importantly of all, can you survive?

Chapter One sets the scene. Then you choose which path to take. Follow the directions at the bottom of each page. The choices you make determine what happens next. After you finish your path, go back and read the others for more adventures.

YOU CHOOSE the path you take through the Cretaceous Period!

Turn the page to begin your adventure.

CHAPTER 1
ONE TOUGH TEST

YOU are taking a test on the Cretaceous Period in science class. The room is silent except for the scratching of pencils. Ms. Turrey is in the back of the room working on a prehistoric terrarium display. Suddenly, you hear some electric pops, and she lets out a startled gasp.

You've always liked Ms. Turrey because she really loves science—and it shows. She's always talking about cool discoveries and cracking science jokes. And she does lots of experiments. Her class is never boring. That's why you don't think much about the noises at first. It's just another one of Ms. Turrey's fun experiments.

But then the room gets humid. A smell comes from the back like mud and leafy plants.

Turn the page.

"Oh my," Ms Turrey says.

You look back. The terrarium contains a model of a Cretaceous Period landscape, complete with plants, toy dinosaurs, and a pool of water representing a sea. For some reason, two big electric cords are attached to the sides of the terrarium. A small gray laptop sits on the table next to it. Its cable has slipped into the fake sea. A gooey liquid sizzles around the computer, eating at the desk. A thick mist wafts from the tank. You drop your pencil.

"Is everything okay?" you ask.

"Please," Ms. Turrey says, "keep working. I'm just going to get the custodian."

She speed walks out. You want to obey her, but your curiosity gets the better of you. You and your best friend, Harriet, go to the now-rumbling tank for a closer look. The mist wraps around you.

"Don't touch anything!" Ms. Turrey calls from the hall. Other students are coming to look too.

Your head suddenly feels strange. Why are you so dizzy? Did the toy Triceratops just look at you? You reach inside the tank to pick it up, and the world spins. You fall back, and when you open your eyes, you're lying on the ground—the muddy ground.

The desks are gone. The tank is gone. Even the walls are gone. Overhead, a pteranodon soars under the sun, dragging its great shadow over you. You don't understand how, but one thing is obvious. You have just been transported to the Cretaceous Period.

To explore a jungle in the Early Cretaceous, turn to page 11.

To wander through a flowery field in the Late Cretaceous, turn to page 41.

To experience the coastline of the sea at the end of the Cretaceous, turn to page 73.

CHAPTER 2

WELCOME TO THE JUNGLE

You wake up on the floor of a forest in a tangle of ferns and other leafy plants. As you open your eyes, you feel a sting on your neck. You slap it, and your hand comes back smeared with blood. The smashed body of a black bug the size of a nickel falls to the dirt by your face. Its legs kick one last time, and it dies.

"What happened?" someone asks.

It's Harriet. She's lying near you in the leaves.

"Ew!" she says, swatting a bug off her hair.

"I can't explain it," you say. "I think we time traveled. It looks like we're in the Cretaceous Period—the Early Cretaceous to be exact."

Turn the page.

"Like on the test," she says.

You're still kneeling on the ground when it begins to rumble. You can feel it through your whole body. Standing up, you look out between the trees and see a herd of huge dinosaurs storming across the plains. Each one is longer than two semitrailers. When they lift their necks, they are taller than your city library—and it's an eight-story building! You know from your science test these are some kind of sauropod. They're not meat eaters, but their sheer size is terrifying. You imagine getting trampled beneath them. There are at least a dozen of them, and each one could use you as a toothpick.

They're heading your way. They are scary, but also fascinating.

To run away, go to the next page.
To hide and watch them, turn to page 15.

"Come on!" you yell.

Harriet follows as you run deeper into the jungle. You leap over a fallen tree. Bugs buzz through the air. A pack of small mammals that you recognize as multituberculates scrambles out of your way and into the brush. They look like rats, but they're the size of house cats.

Finally, the rumbling fades behind you. It's getting dark, and the breeze is chilly. You realize you had better start thinking about shelter. Where is a safe place to sleep? You worry about sleeping on the ground, where any dinosaur or animal could reach you. You look up at the tree in front of you. It is choked with moss, twisty vines, and fern leaves, making the upper branches almost impossible to see into.

"I think we should find a tree where we can spend the night," you say.

Turn the page.

"I'm hungry," Harriet replies.

"Well I don't think we're going to find a cheeseburger tonight. We need to get somewhere safe until morning."

You and Harriet find a tree with a good strong limb and a thick curtain of leaves to keep you hidden. You gather some leaves and vines to keep you as warm as possible, but still you shiver all through the night.

The next morning, Harriet stretches and looks around. She looks exhausted. You know you probably look the same.

"Now about that cheeseburger," Harriet says.

You know she's just kidding. But she is also right—you need food.

To try to catch a multituberculate, turn to page 18.
To eat plants, turn to page 21.

The dinosaurs would crush you like a bug. But they are so beautiful! You've never seen a living thing so large and yet so graceful. No human ever has! You decide to stay in the jungle and watch them.

You and Harriet hide behind a tree and watch. The sauropods lumber toward you. Your heart races, but you hold your position. Then the herd stops and starts eating. One of the incredible beasts prods its long neck in the canopy of trees just above you and pulls off a mouthful of leaves. Its biting and swallowing sounds like a washing machine cycle. Specks of saliva and broken branches fall onto your head. You watch in amazement.

Suddenly, the herd stops eating. They all sense you—you must be mysterious to them. Just as quickly as they came, they leave. The earth rumbles for a few minutes, and then they are gone.

Turn the page.

"That was awesome!" Harriet whispers.

You agree. No matter what you get on your science test, this has been worth it. You are still thinking about the sauropods when you slap an itch on your arm. It's another big black bug. The air buzzes with flying insects, and you wave your hands to shoo them away.

"I hate these bugs!" Harriet says. "Let's get out of the trees. It looks like there aren't as many out in the sunshine."

"I hate them too," you say. "But what about dinosaurs? And other predators? We'd have nowhere to hide out there. We're probably safer in the jungle."

To stay in the jungle, turn to page 25.
To go out onto the plains, turn to page 27.

You think it would be a lot easier to grab some plants than it would be to catch a quick animal. But looking around, it's hard to tell which plants are safe. You know that some plants are toxic to humans. In prehistoric times, maybe all of them are.

"Okay," you say. "Let's give it a shot."

You find a long stick on the ground and sharpen it by scraping it against a rough boulder. Eventually you have a deadly spear. Harriet goes around a stand of shrubs where some of the multituberculates are hiding. She raises her arms and storms toward them.

"Raar!" she yells.

Several of the furry creatures run out of the bushes, right toward you. They flash their sharp little teeth at you, and you jump out of the way.

"Yikes!" you cry.

"Hey," Harriet says. "You have to do better than that!"

"Sorry," you say. "Let's try it again.

Harriet finds another multituberculate and scares it toward you. This time you don't falter. You stab at it with your spear, but you miss. You repeat the process countless more times—the little mammals are everywhere. Finally, you stick one.

"Thank goodness," Harriet says. "I'm starving."

Using your sharpened stick, you skin the creature and pull off the meat.

"Wait," you say. "How can we make a fire? We don't have any matches or anything."

Turn the page.

"Let's just eat it," Harriet says.

She's staring at the meat and licking her lips. You've noticed that she's started acting more and more primitive since you got here. Being trapped in the Cretaceous Period is turning her into some kind of cavewoman.

To eat it raw, turn to page 28.
To try to make a fire, turn to page 32.

You don't want to deal with trying to catch and cook an animal. Gross! Besides, you know a little bit about what is safe to eat in the forest—assuming the prehistoric forest is similar to a modern forest.

"Look for some green balls," you say. "Like tennis balls. They should have nuts inside."

"What about these leaves?" Harriet says, pulling some small bunches from the dirt. "They look like parsley."

"Don't!" you say. "They might be toxic." You scan the trees and find a few green balls. "Here, break these open."

You and Harriet collect more green balls and break them open against a big rock. Soon you are eating a nice meal of nuts. Next, you follow the sloping forest downhill until you find a stream.

Turn the page.

You both take long drinks. The water tastes delicious and fresh.

You freeze when you hear a deafening shriek. Mammals, lizards, snakes, and other creatures are running away from the water back into the forest. Birds rise out of the trees and flee into the sky. What are they afraid of?

When you look up from the water, you get your answer. A dinosaur stands on two giant legs on the other side of the stream, maybe 100 feet away. It towers 20 feet high and has a tall, spiny sail along its back. Its head is longer than your whole body. And when it opens its massive jaws, you see plenty of spiky teeth.

Harriet gasps. "Spinosaurus," she whispers.

"Oh no!" you say. "Those are meat eaters."

"And we are meat," she replies.

Turn the page.

You're terrified! So you do what a terrified person would do. You run. As soon as you start running, the Spinosaurus gives chase. It splashes across the stream. It crashes up the bank on your side. It huffs and barks.

You run faster than you ever thought you could. Harriet is right next to you. But it is no use. You feel the beast's hot breath on your back. You know that your time in the Cretaceous Period has come to an end.

THE END

To follow another path, turn to page 9.
To learn more about the Cretaceous Period, turn to page 103.

"I think we're safer in here," you say. "A few bug bites won't kill us, right?"

"I don't know about that," Harriet says.

She follows you into the jungle anyway. It is an amazing world. A thick tree canopy blots out the sky. Vines, leafy plants, snakes, and little mammals are everywhere. But the bugs are really bad.

"Let's find a stream or river," Harriet says. "If we can find some mud, we can rub it on our skin to keep the bugs off."

You search for over an hour, eventually finding a stream. You each coat your bodies with mud. You even manage to laugh at how silly you look. But it seems to be a little too late. The bug bites you already have are very itchy. You scratch at them with growing intensity.

Turn the page.

Soon you are bleeding, and the bites are swelling. You begin to feel very thirsty. But drinking water barely helps.

"Either our scratches are infected, or those bugs were poisonous," Harriet says.

"This is really bad," you agree.

Harriet is the first to throw up. You join her shortly. Blood is streaming out of your bug bites, your stomach is twisting, and you feel very hot. You have a fever. You shut your eyes. You thought dinosaurs were your biggest threat here, but it turns out insects will be the death of you.

THE END

To follow another path, turn to page 9.
To learn more about the Cretaceous Period, turn to page 103.

"I'll take my chances with predators," Harriet says. "These bugs are going to eat us alive!"

"Okay, okay," you reply.

The two of you scramble out of the jungle and onto the open land. You walk through sauropod footprints bigger than sidewalk squares. You still get a few bug bites, but way fewer than before. As the sun sets behind the mountains, a beautiful orange and pink light settles over the plains.

You follow a stream until you reach a bay. Farther out, a giant sea opens up.

"I think we can spend the night here. It seems safe. Look—there's a little cave where we can stay dry and hidden."

"I think I'd feel better if we made some kind of weapon to protect ourselves first," Harriet says.

To head to the cave, turn to page 35.
To make a weapon first, turn to page 38.

You're not sure you could start a fire, so you start tearing apart the strange primitive mammals. But once you bite into the meat, your stomach turns.

"I don't think I can do it," you say, holding the meat away from your face.

"Me neither," Harriet says. "What if there's some kind of prehistoric disease in the meat?"

You toss the meat into the bushes. The bushes rustle in reaction. Something is moving in there.

"Uh, Harriet?" you say.

"I see it," she answers.

You freeze and wait. A dinosaur about the size of a large dog steps out of the bushes on its hind legs. It has a short, beaked snout and strong upper legs with fingerlike claws.

The animal hisses, and you jump back. You recognize it as a Hypsilophodon.

"Don't worry," you whisper. "It's a plant eater."

"I'm not feeling very comforted by that for some reason," she responds.

The creature looks behind you. You hear a low, raspy growl and turn around. In a nearby clearing stands another two-legged dinosaur, only this one is much bigger. It has a big, gaping jaw and sharp teeth. A tall sail of spines sticks up on its back.

"I know this one," Harriet says. "It was the answer to the second question on the test. It's an Acrocanthosaurus."

"Plant eater?" you ask hopefully.

"Nope."

Turn the page.

The Hypsilophodon is off and running. It looks like a kangaroo bounding along, and it's really fast. You can hear the Acrocanthosaurus breathing hard as it advances. It reaches the edge of the clearing and rams into a tree with its shoulder. The tree creaks and gives way. If it can get through the trees, it will get to you.

You and Harriet run. You hear the big tree crash. Then another tree crashes. The giant footsteps of the meat-eating monster get closer and closer. Harriet screams as it scoops her up. You know you're next. Your time in the Cretaceous Period has come to an end.

THE END

To follow another path, turn to page 9.
To learn more about the Cretaceous Period, turn to page 103.

"I'm not eating this thing raw," you say. "Let's see if we can make a fire."

You gather some dried leaves and bark and pile it up. You rub two sticks together for a long time. Your hands get tired, and you let Harriet take a turn. The sticks get warm. But that's the best you can do. The wood is too damp to catch fire. You don't eat the creature.

After a little searching, you find a nest of dinosaur eggs. You're not crazy about the idea of eating raw eggs, but it's not as disgusting as eating raw meat. You take an egg and crack it into your mouth. It is slimy and cool, but somehow you manage to get it down. You feel some strength seeping back into your body.

Over several days, you keep an eye on the nesting area. A community of Hypsilophodons come and go, checking their eggs.

The animals are the size of large dogs.
Each one has a thick, long tail and a stout,
beaked head. You know from science class that
they're plant eaters.

You and Harriet start gathering wood and
laying it in the sun to dry. After many attempts
rubbing the dry sticks together, you finally get a
few sparks. You manage to build a fire and keep
it going all the time. It helps keep the bugs away.

Harriet makes a sling from vines and a stick,
which she uses to fire rocks. With that, she hunts
the multituberculate. You use sharp sticks and
rocks to skin them and cook them over the fire.

When you gather water at the stream, you
see flamingo-like pterosaurs. They are
Pterodaustros, and they are peaceful and
beautiful. They use long, scooped beaks to strain
tiny shrimp in the shallows.

Turn the page.

Fish are coming to eat the swarms of tiny shrimp. That gives you an idea. You sharpen a spear so that you can fish.

Weeks pass, then months. You have created a tasty tea from roots and leaves you gather near your tree shelter. You eat fish, small mammals, nuts, and berries. You know the hunting patterns of the meat-eating dinosaurs, so you can easily avoid them. You tell each other stories about life back home, and sometimes you even crack jokes. It turns out you are good at living in the Early Cretaceous Period. Even though you miss home, you kind of like it here.

THE END

To follow another path, turn to page 9.
To learn more about the Cretaceous Period, turn to page 103.

"I want to get out of the open as quick as possible," you say. "It's almost dark, and we're sitting ducks."

The two of you climb down the rocks and into the entryway of the small cave. You are surprised by how easy it is to fall asleep in spite of the crazy situation. You must really be tired. Early in the morning you hear some yipping animals up above.

"Don't move," Harriet whispers.

Whatever is up there, it's better if they don't know you're here. After a while, the yipping fades away. You climb out of the cave and back up the bank.

Far across the beach near the jungle you see a pack of Deinonychuses galloping across the land. These birdlike dinosaurs are your favorite.

Turn the page.

The Deinonychuses are about 10 feet long. Their bodies and long tails are covered in feathers. Though you can't see it from here, you know that each one has deadly claws on its feet. They are beautiful creatures, but they are meat eaters. They are vicious and scary.

"I'm glad they didn't find us," Harriet says.

You look back toward the cave, where a thick mist has formed over the water. It looks familiar.

"Hey, remember Ms. Turrey's terrarium?"

Harriet looks too. "It looks just like that scene. No Triceratops, though."

That's when you remember the toy Triceratops in your hoodie pocket. You pull it out. You and Harriet climb back down the bank and into the mist. As you do, the mist begins to swirl around you.

You get dizzy and fall down, but you don't fall into water. Instead, you're lying on the hard floor of Ms. Turrey's classroom.

"Whoa, are you two okay?" someone says. It's your friend Luis.

"We're fine," you say, though you're not totally sure that's true. You certainly feel weird.

"You better get back in your seat," Luis says. "I hear Ms. Turrey coming back."

"Yes," you say as your eyes connect with Harriet's. "I guess we should finish that test."

THE END

To follow another path, turn to page 9.
To learn more about the Cretaceous Period, turn to page 103.

You agree that it's better to have something to defend yourselves. Who knows what kind of creatures are out here. You're looking for a branch to use as a club or a long stick you can sharpen into a spear. As you search, you lose sight of Harriet.

You find a stick that can be sharpened into a short spear and head back toward the cave. As you draw near, you hear the sound of animals galloping. Near the cave, dozens of Deinonychuses are running across the beach. You know about these dinosaurs. They're 10 feet long and fast. They have teeth like steak knives and strong arms and legs. And they have a long, deadly claw on each foot. Covered in feathers, they look like giant birds—if birds could tear you to shreds.

"Help!" Harriet screams.

She is running toward you, and the Deinonychuses are following. You turn to run, but it's too late. First they catch Harriet. Then they catch you. You flail your stick at them, but it's no use.

THE END

To follow another path, turn to page 9.
To learn more about the Cretaceous Period, turn to page 103.

CHAPTER 3

ALL THE BEAUTIFUL FLOWERS

You look around to find that you're in a field of flowering bushes, trees, and vines. The area is full of dazzling colors. The sun beats down on you, and immediately you begin to sweat.

You become aware of an intense buzzing. It's not just your head aching. There are millions of enormous bees, mosquitoes, and other flying, buzzing bugs you've never seen before. The insects dip and land on bright, beautiful flowers. Then they rise again and dip back, over and over. Some of them are as large as hummingbirds. The air is cloudy with them.

Turn the page.

Lying next to you are two friends from class, Harriet and Luis. There is no sign of Ms. Turrey, no sign of the terrarium from her room, and no sign of any of your other classmates. You realize Luis and Harriet must have grabbed onto you at the moment you went back in time. That's why they got pulled back with you. In the distance, a couple of looming volcanoes pipe out puffs of smoke. And across the field is a huge, duck-billed dinosaur munching happily on some plants. It has a colorful crest on top of its head.

"Whoa! What happened?" Luis says. "I hope this is part of the test!"

"Uh, I don't think it is, Luis," Harriet says. She's holding your science book open in her hands and comparing what she reads to what she sees all around. "I think we've landed in the Late Cretaceous Period."

"Amazing," you say.

You're still holding the toy Triceratops from Ms. Turrey's terrarium in your hand. You shove it into the pocket of your hoodie just as it starts to rain. It's just a sprinkle at first, but dark clouds hint at a bigger storm coming soon.

"It's sunny up on that mountain," Harriet says. "Maybe we can get up there where it's dry."

"The jungle is closer," Luis says, "and the canopy of trees will keep us dry. Kind of."

"Jungles have lots of snakes and other creatures," Harriet says.

One thing is for sure. If you wait much longer, you're going to be totally soaked.

To make a run for the mountain, turn the page.
To head for the jungle, turn to page 47.

The mountain might be far away, but the jungle sounds creepy. You start running up the incline, hoping to get out of the rain. It's not long before you stop in your tracks. That's because the duck-billed dinosaur has stopped eating and lifted its head. It stands perfectly still and looks toward the mountain.

"It's some kind of Lambeosaur," Luis says. "It's super cool, but we need to keep moving."

"Hold on," you say. That Lambeosaur is still frozen. Something is wrong. "Why isn't it moving? What does it sense?"

"You guys," Harriet says. "My book is getting wet. We might need this."

Suddenly, the Lambeosaur lets out a loud honking sound, like a deep siren. It is warning its herd that a threat is coming.

Turn the page.

When it begins running down the mountain, dozens of other Lambeosaurs come out of the surrounding hills and trees. They all run downhill.

"I think something's up there," you say.

To follow the Lambeosaurs, turn to page 49.

To keep heading up the mountain, turn to page 52.

By the time you reach the trees, you're already quite wet. But under the canopy, the rain doesn't reach you. You sit down against a tree trunk and ask Harriet if there's anything in the science book that can explain what happened to you.

"No," Harriet says, "there is definitely nothing in here about time travel."

Near your head, a flowery branch begins to twitch. You look closer. Hanging upside down beneath the leaves, a colony of flies wriggle. Each one is at least an inch long. They seem to be looking at you. You look closer. They have big, sharp jaws. Large, upside-down flying creatures with sharp teeth? Sounds a little too much like vampires to you.

"Let's get away from these things," you say.

"Those are crane flies," Harriet says.

Turn the page.

"I don't care what they are," you say. "Let's go."

The three of you start walking away, but some of the flies follow you. You wave your hands at them and start to run. Eventually you stop in a clearing to catch your breath.

That's when something grabs onto your foot. It's a massive snake.

To try to pull away, turn to page 55.
To look for a weapon, turn to page 58.

A predator is coming! Your instincts tell you to run with the Lambeosaurs. Maybe you can hide among them. Odds are whatever is coming will pick one of them instead of you.

You run after the big, duck-billed dinosaurs. They are all shrieking and honking now. Combined with their earth-shaking steps, the sound is terrifying. And those big dinosaurs are fast! You can't keep up. The plants are high, slowing you down. Soon you, Harriet, and Luis fall behind. The Lambeosaurs thunder ahead, and you are getting tired.

Breathing hard, you slow down and look over your shoulder. You shudder to see a Tyrannosaurus rex storming toward you. It's catching up very quickly, and now Luis has fallen down.

Turn the page.

Suddenly the sky ignites! A bolt of lightning strikes the field. There's an ear-shattering crack of thunder just a half second after. The flowers smolder, then go up in flames. Even in the rain, a fire begins to rage.

To keep running, turn to page 60.
To go back for Luis, turn to page 64.

"If something is chasing those Lambeosaurs, I don't want to be around when it catches them," Harriet says.

You agree. Let the Lambeosaurs be dinner, not you! They'll all be extinct soon anyway.

You run up the mountain. The flowers are mashed down in a line, making a faint path through the field, and you follow it. You realize—too late—that there can be only one reason for a path. Something walks that way a lot. You are still thinking about this when Luis grabs onto your shoulder.

"What?" you ask.

He puts his hand over your mouth and points. Up ahead is a Tyrannosaurus rex. Standing tall on its massive hind legs, it looks bigger than a house.

It opens its gigantic jaws. Its teeth look like enormous daggers ready to slice flesh. Drool streams from its mouth.

It turns one red eye on you and leans forward. Suddenly it lunges downhill toward you. Before you can think of what to do, Harriet grabs your hand and pulls you between some boulders. You crouch there, hidden in a tight space. The T. rex bangs its head against the rocks. You can smell its swampy breath. The boulders shake, but the T. rex can't get through—for now.

The giant beast lunges again at the rocks, and this time Harriet stabs at its eye with a big stick. It flinches and rears up. The T. rex roars angrily and crashes its head against the rocks again. You can feel them moving. This hiding spot won't hold for very long.

Turn the page.

You're suddenly distracted, though, as the volcano you've been climbing belches up a huge cloud of smoke. The earth rumbles, and the T. rex turns its attention to the present danger. It seems now more concerned about its own survival than eating you.

To stay hidden from the T. rex, turn to page 66.

To get away from the volcano, turn to page 69.

Your instincts take over. All you can think to do is pull, pull, pull. You try to get away.

"Help!" you yell.

Harriet finds a big rock and smashes it on the snake. You feel its muscles flinch against your leg and you pull again. You are loose for half a second, but then the snake rewraps. It gets farther up your leg. You scream again for help.

Luis is pulling its tail, trying to separate you. But the huge snake is too strong. Then it twists up around your waist. It's getting hard to breathe. Harriet hits it again and again, but it doesn't help. The snake wraps around your chest. It wraps around your neck. It opens its big mouth.

You can't breathe.

Turn the page.

Your friends are screaming. It squeezes even harder.

You can't breathe.

It hisses into your ear.

You can't—

THE END

To follow another path, turn to page 9.
To learn more about the Cretaceous Period, turn to page 103.

You fall to the ground. Near your face is a rock the size of a softball, and you grab it. Whack! The snake hisses. Just then, something scurries under the brush nearby. You feel the snake's grip relax as a brown mammal the size of a beaver steps out of the bushes. You know these from your test: multituberculates. Just as quickly as it grabbed you, the snake releases you and slithers after the mammal.

Luis says, "Thank goodness that thing looked like an easier meal than you."

You sit on the ground catching your breath. Your friends sit next to you and hug you, and you realize you've been crying. You almost died.

While you rest, Luis searches the area for water or something to eat. Harriet stays with you. For a second you think it's a bad idea to separate. But then you fall asleep.

When you wake up, it's dark. You're not sure where you are. Was the Cretaceous just a dream? You rub your eyes and look into the darkness around you. A figure is standing there. You think maybe you are home in bed.

"Mom?" you say.

The figure moves, and you realize it's not a person. It's a dinosaur about the size of an adult man. It walks on hind legs and has a hard, flat skull with spines on it. Next to you, Harriet grabs onto your arm.

"Oh no," she says.

It's a Pachycephalosaur. The spines on its skull are the last thing you see as it charges toward you.

THE END

To follow another path, turn to page 9.
To learn more about the Cretaceous Period, turn to page 103.

Luis scrambles into the tall weeds to hide. Smoke is spreading fast, and it's hard to see. The duck-billed dinosaurs wail their wild horn sounds. The T. rex growls and stomps. Holding hands so you don't get separated, you and Harriet run through the smoke, calling for Luis as you go. Soon the sounds of the dinosaurs fade.

Eventually you reach a lake. You're worried about Luis, but you don't dare go back toward the fire. Besides the flames, there's also that T. rex. You just hope Luis has found a safe place to hide.

Through the smoke you see one of your favorite dinosaurs: a Dracorex hogwartsia. Named after a character from your favorite book series, it is a plant eater with a hard, flat skull, spiky horns, and a long muzzle. It trots away when it sees you.

Turn the page.

When you gaze back down into the water, you see Ms. Turrey's classroom. The lake water combines with the pool of misty water inside the terrarium.

"I think this must be the portal home," Harriet says.

Overjoyed, you reach into your hoodie and pull out the toy Triceratops. You take Harriet's hand again and step into the lake.

"Wait!" Harriet says. Right as she speaks, you feel the world spin.

When you open your eyes again, you're in the classroom. Your friends are looking at you in amazement. You're home! But your happiness quickly fades when you see Harriet's troubled face.

"I said, 'Wait!'"

"Why?" you say.

But then you realize why. You left Luis behind. A sick feeling comes over you. How will you live with the knowledge that you abandoned him?

THE END

To follow another path, turn to page 9.
To learn more about the Cretaceous Period, turn to page 103.

"We have to help Luis!" you say.

The two of you run up the mountain toward the T. rex. The fire spreads quickly. The flames rage dangerously close. All sorts of creatures are dashing past you—mammals, lizards, and snakes. Birds are flying away from the mountain. The insects have disappeared.

"Luis!" Harriet screams.

"Luis!" you scream.

There's no answer. You keep searching. Dinosaurs run past you. Some are the size of big dogs. Some are the size of people. Some are much bigger. You dodge the great legs of the T. rex. Maybe it's not even the same one. Four-legged dinosaurs also run past. All the creatures are terrified, running for their lives. Flames rise into the sky.

The smoke makes it hard to breathe and to see. Something knocks you to the ground. Pain races up your arm into your shoulder. Your hand dangles like something dead—your wrist is broken. But you have worse problems. Something large steps on your leg and crushes the bones. You can't get up. You can't see. You don't know where your friends are.

You curl up and cover your head. You hope Luis and Harriet will survive, even though you will not.

THE END

To follow another path, turn to page 9.
To learn more about the Cretaceous Period, turn to page 103.

Is the volcano erupting? You're not sure. But you are sure that there is a T. rex out there somewhere. You tell Luis and Harriet that it feels safer here, where at least you won't be eaten.

"Good point," Luis says.

You hunch behind the rocks and wait. You keep watch from your cove, but you do not see the T. rex anymore.

It was already hot, but now it's getting much hotter. All three of you are sweating. Something is crackling. You look out from the rocks and see lava streaming down the mountain. Trees and bushes and all those flowering plants are going up in flames.

"Um, you guys?" you say. "I think we better get out of here."

"I think you're right," Harriet says.

Turn the page.

You jump out of the rocks and start running downhill as fast as you can. Looking behind you, you see a fresh lava stream lapping at the earth. You trip over a big tree root and get the wind knocked out of you. Luis turns and lifts you up. The air is scorching hot. You run to catch up to Harriet. But the lava is coming too fast. You were worried about making it home, but you won't even make it to the bottom of this mountain.

THE END

To follow another path, turn to page 9.
To learn more about the Cretaceous Period, turn to page 103.

"I think this volcano is erupting," Harriet says nervously.

"We better get out of here!" Luis cries.

"What about that T. rex?" you ask.

"She's smart," Harriet replies. "She's running away from the volcano!"

You climb out of the rocky hideout and run down the mountain. Fat streams of lava seem to chase you. The sky is darkening as the volcano belches black smoke. The flowery field catches fire. Nearly out of breath, you get off the mountain just in time.

You run until you reach a lake with a wide, muddy beach. Walking along the shore, you find a cave that seems safe from the fire. The three of you climb inside and wait. You drink some fresh water from a stream that trickles down the wall.

Turn the page.

A few days later, the fire dies down. You climb out of the cave and look around. The landscape is smoking and barren.

You walk all day looking for food. You find some nuts and a tree with yellow fruits on it. You're so hungry that everything tastes amazing.

Days pass. Then weeks. You and your friends make a home in the cave by the lake. You collect nuts and fruits, and soon you have a large store of food.

"Do you think Ms. Turrey knows where we are?" you ask one day.

"I hope so," Luis says. "Maybe she'll get us home."

In the meantime, you have gotten very good at surviving in the Cretaceous Period. You know you can wait a long time, if you have to.

THE END

To follow another path, turn to page 9.
To learn more about the Cretaceous Period, turn to page 103.

CHAPTER 4

SEAFOOD SPECIAL

You stand up in the mud and take a step forward. But there is nowhere for your foot to land. You fall off a cliff and splash into frigid water. The mist thickens around you. You shiver.

"Hello?" you call.

"Over here!" someone says.

"Luis? Is that you?"

"It's me!" he says.

You swim toward the voice. Finally, you find him. His lips are trembling and turning blue. It sure is cold!

"We have to get out of this water!" you say. "I fell off a cliff around here somewhere."

Turn the page.

"Let's swim this way," Luis says.

You follow him through the mist, which is quickly turning into rain. A strip of land appears out of the gloom, and you crawl up onto the beach. You're both lying in the mud catching your breath.

"You okay?" you ask.

"I'm okay," Luis says. "You?"

"I'm good."

You get up and walk up the beach toward a rocky outcropping you can barely see through the mist. You find a place to hide under the rocks until the rain stops. When it does, the sun comes out, and the temperature spikes. You start sweating. You step out of the rocks into the blazing sun. Your clothes dry out quickly. You're so hot you almost wish they'd stayed wet.

You look around. You're on a small rocky island. About 50 yards across the lagoon is a larger landmass where you can see fruit trees. You peer into the water and see a school of giant rays, even bigger than manta rays, swimming past.

To swim for the large landmass, turn the page.

To explore your island, turn to page 79.

You and Luis decide to swim for the shore. The rays swim beneath you. You look into the water and watch them glide right below you. They're as big as cars! Luckily, they don't seem to mind you swimming with them.

When you reach the beach, you and Luis scramble up out of the water as fast as you can. You lay in the sun drying off for a few minutes.

You're about to go check out the fruit on the nearby trees when you hear a loud squawk. In the trees at the top of the beach, a dinosaur stares at you. It reminds you of an ostrich. It has a long, sharp beak and feathers all over. Its arms and legs have long claws. You freeze. You think this is a Troodon. You remember studying them in school. Troodons likely ate both plants and animals. Though they probably hunted small animals, you still don't like the way it's looking at you.

Turn the page.

The Troodon raises its wings to scare you. It works. As you back away toward the water, you bump into Luis.

"Better stop," he says.

You turn around. He's staring at a 10-foot crocodile at the edge of the water. It opens its big jaws and claps them shut.

To go toward the Troodon, turn to page 82.
To go toward the crocodile, turn to page 84.

"Let's not get back in that water," you say, pointing to the giant rays. "I feel safer here."

"I agree," Luis says.

You scout the island looking for fresh water and shelter. You walk through a swampy stand of trees and come out at a cliff edge. This must be where you fell off when you first arrived. Birds and several pteranodons soar overhead. Out over the water, you hear splashes and churning waves.

What is creating this ruckus? A giant head rises out of the water on a long, powerful neck. A sauropod wades through the water and begins chomping on some trees nearby.

The sauropod has a beardlike frill on its throat. You recognize it as an Alamosaurus. Compared to it, you feel like an ant.

Turn the page.

Luis gasps, and the massive creature startles. It looks at you for a second, then lifts its tail out of the water. It's like a massive oak trunk, except it flexes like a whip.

The tail thrashes into the water and a giant wave pounds up onto the island and knocks you down. You get up, and the tail swings again. This time it's coming right at you. Luis jumps into the water. You're not sure if that's a good idea, but then neither is staying here.

To join Luis in the water, turn to page 86.
To hide behind the trees for protection, turn to page 88.

No way are you going to let some prehistoric crocodile take a shot at you. You run up the beach toward the Troodon. It opens its wings again and squawks. You know that croc is lumbering after you, so you keep charging ahead. The Troodon turns and runs off along the sand.

You look back. The crocodile chased you halfway up the beach, but now it sits and looks at you. It's a fast sprinter, but those short legs make it hard to run that quickly for a long time. It just snaps its jaws at you a couple times, then turns to waddle back to the water. All the muscles in your body relax when you realize you're safe—for now. Your heart is still pounding as you turn your attention to the trees.

"Look at these enormous fruits," you say.

Luis joins you at the tree and you shake a branch until a couple of orange fruits fall down. They're as big as coconuts with a soft, fleshy peel. You poke your thumb into the top of one and rip it open. It tastes like honey and orange.

"Amazing!" Luis says.

You each eat one of the fruits. Then you have another. You are relaxing in the sand with full bellies when you hear something rustling in the bushes. It's coming from deep in the jungle. It sounds slow. And it sounds big. The sun is getting low in the sky, meaning night is coming soon. A fire could keep you warm and scare away predators. On the other hand, you might want to find out just what's out there.

To try to build a fire on the beach, turn to page 90.
To investigate, turn to page 92.

You know the Troodon is not likely to hunt you. Even if there's a pack of them, you are too big. But somehow it seems too scary to get any closer. At least a crocodile is something you've seen before.

So you linger on the beach. Luis keeps an eye on the croc, and you watch the Troodon.

"He's coming closer," Luis warns.

"More Troodons are coming out of the woods," you say.

"He's coming closer," Luis says again.

You turn to look. The croc is stepping slowly and surely toward you. You look back to the Troodons. Suddenly, they all squawk and run away.

"Let's go!" Luis says as he runs past you.

You start running, but the croc latches onto your foot. You try to twist away, but its jaws are too powerful. Your leg is crushed. The croc is pulling you backward toward the water.

"Luis!" you yell.

Your fingers rake lines in the sand, trying to hold your ground. Luis comes and kicks the crocodile in the belly, but it doesn't do any good. In a few seconds, it has pulled you under the water.

THE END

To follow another path, turn to page 9.
To learn more about the Cretaceous Period, turn to page 103.

It's best to stick together, even if this is crazy! You jump off the cliff and plunge back into the cold water. You stay underwater and swim in the opposite direction of the Alamosaurus. Even underwater, you hear its giant tail hitting the island. When you finally surface, you look up. The place where you were standing is rubble.

"Luis!" you call out. "Luis, where are you?"

Finally, you see Luis swimming toward the mainland. You swim after him. Suddenly a fish almost as long as a minivan swims upward toward you. It has gaping, sharp-looking buck teeth. It's a Xiphactinus, and it opens its mouth to chomp you. It looks like your time in the Cretaceous Period is over. You only hope Luis finds a way to survive.

THE END

To follow another path, turn to page 9.
To learn more about the Cretaceous Period, turn to page 103.

You turn and run toward the other side of the island. The tail crashes onto the cliff and smashes trees and rocks, which crumble into the sea. It is an awesome sight. You push through the thick branches and leaves. Once you arrive at the other side of the island, you climb down to the beach where you and Luis first came up. He is there in the mud waiting for you.

"Let's get off this island," you say. "And away from that big guy."

"Good call," Luis says.

You begin to swim back across the lagoon. Your limbs are tired, and your heart is racing furiously. You still haven't caught your breath, and you're afraid you won't make it to the island in the distance. Luis looks pretty tired too.

You're both beginning to flounder when a giant sea turtle surfaces nearby. It's bigger than a van.

"I don't know if I can swim much more," Luis gasps. "Maybe we should get a ride on that guy."

"He seems pretty relaxed," you reply. "It might be our best shot.

Luis climbs onto its back, and you join him. You both lean up and grab onto the collar of its shell.

The turtle drags you to the mainland, without even seeming to notice you're there. As you get close to land, you slip off into the water and wade ashore.

"I'm tired of being wet and cold," Luis says.

"Me too," you agree. "Let's build a fire."

Turn the page.

You quickly gather dried twigs, leaves, and grass, while Luis clears out a shallow hole. Luis takes off his watch and breaks the glass off the face. He holds it so it captures the sun's rays and concentrates them on the pile of kindling. It's not long before the grass and leaves begin to smoke, and Luis blows on them gently. Soon, you have bright flames.

You gather bigger twigs and dry sun-bleached driftwood. Before long, evening is upon you, and your fire is raging.

Suddenly, you hear a series of loud cracks coming from the forest. A large tree tumbles over and lands in the sand near your fire. An Ankylosaurus comes out of the woods after it. The tank-shaped dinosaur stops to munch on the leaves of the tree, which are now conveniently at ground level.

It looks at you. Its tail looks like a stone beach ball attached to the end of a whip. You gulp nervously as it swishes that club of a tail around like a happy house cat. To your relief, it eats all the leaves and moves on.

After it's gone, you're still not alone. More monsters lurk in the woods. You hear them snorting, pushing through the leaves, and occasionally growling or yelping at one another. Maybe you should find something to defend yourself with, but you don't really want to leave the comforting glow of the fire.

To spend the night by your fire, turn to page 94.
To look for a weapon, turn to page 98.

You don't want any surprises in the middle of the night. You slip into the trees for a look around. You follow the noises—chomping, snorting, and snuffling. A tree cracks and falls. You hear a deep, rasping cough, and then out of the darkness shuffles an Ankylosaurus. For a moment, you and Luis are in a staring contest with the massive turtlelike dinosaur. Then you see something change in its eyes. Fear. It's never seen a human before. You almost laugh at the thought of this monstrous beast being afraid of you.

It turns—much quicker than you would think such a big animal could do—and suddenly its big tail is whizzing through the air. The end of the tail is a giant, hard ball with spikes. It crushes you and Luis in a single blow.

THE END

To follow another path, turn to page 9.
To learn more about the Cretaceous Period, turn to page 103.

You and Luis take turns collecting wood nearby and stoking the fire all through the night. In the morning, you wake up on the beach under the baking sun.

You're barely awake when you hear a deep snort behind you. You turn and see a Triceratops walking across the beach. From up on a berm, an Albertosaurus climbs down toward you as well. This quick theropod is a lot like a T. rex, but smaller. It has its eyes on the Triceratops.

The Triceratops does not intend to become anyone's dinner today. It lowers its head and charges, goring its enemy with one of its long, spear-like tusks. The Albertosaurus screams, and the sand around it darkens with blood.

The Triceratops turns and looks at you. You should probably be scared, but for some reason, you're not. You recall the toy Triceratops in Ms. Turrey's terrarium.

"Hi," you say.

"Are you kidding me?" Luis asks. "Talking to a dinosaur? He just gored that other guy."

"I think it wants us to follow it," you say.

You grab Luis's arm and pull him after the Triceratops. He follows along reluctantly. The beast leads you down the beach to a rocky pool at the edge of the lagoon. A mist hovers over the water. It looks like the terrarium. You step past the Triceratops. You can't explain it, but you trust the dinosaur.

Turn the page.

Dragging Luis, you step into the misty pool. The air begins to swirl. Then a powerful wind kicks in. When it settles, you are standing in the classroom next to the terrarium.

"Students, please sit down," Ms. Turrey says.

"What?" you say, still trying to take in the sudden shift in surroundings.

"I'm glad you like my diorama," she says, "but you do have a test to finish."

With a sigh of relief, you go back to your desk. You've never been so happy to take a test in your life.

THE END

To follow another path, turn to page 9.
To learn more about the Cretaceous Period, turn to page 103.

There's no way you'll be able to sleep here anyway, so you walk along the beach looking for something to throw or swing at a predator. You also gather wood to burn.

Somehow you survive the night. Over the next several days you collect rocks to throw, fruits and roots to eat, and wood for the fire. You and Luis take turns eating and foraging. It is a boring life, but you are alive. That is all you care about for now.

Then one day you are lying on the beach looking at the sky when you see a raging ball of fire plummet from space. It screams and crackles louder than anything you've ever heard. The sky turns an amazing purple and yellow as the asteroid crashes into Earth far, south of you.

Turn the page.

"That's the asteroid," Luis says. His face is streaked with mud. His eyes and skin are red from sunburn. His shirt is torn and bloody. "The one that hits Chicxulub."

"The one that killed the dinosaurs?" you say.

"That's the one."

Over the next few hours, you watch as the sky to the south grows dark with smoke and ash. You know that massive waves will make their way across miles and miles of ocean, crash onto land, and flood it. You can't see much of the destruction yet, but you know it is coming. You can smell the smoke. Fires are coming.

"We're going to die here," you say. "We're going to die in the Cretaceous Period."

"I'm afraid you're right," Luis says.

He doesn't look scared or worried. You've been barely surviving for so many weeks by now. You've fought off dinosaurs and other prehistoric animals. You've wondered if you'd ever see your families again. Maybe a quick death is the best you can hope for.

THE END

To follow another path, turn to page 9.
To learn more about the Cretaceous Period, turn to page 103.

CHAPTER 5

THE CRETACEOUS PERIOD

The Cretaceous Period was dominated by dinosaurs and ended with their extinction. It started about 145 million years ago, following the Jurassic Period, and lasted about 79 million years. During this time, Earth was reshaping itself as the supercontinent Pangea drifted apart. By the end of the period, oceans had filled in the gaps between continents, which looked a lot like they do now. Temperatures all over the globe were warmer than they are now.

One of the most important features of the Cretaceous Period was the development of flowering plants. They spread across the land, and flying insects such as bees and wasps pollinated them. Other insects, such as butterflies, ants, beetles, and grasshoppers, also spread.

Ancestors of many modern bird types appeared during this period, including cormorants, pelicans, and sandpipers. Mammals, especially multituberculates, lived comfortably in the forests. Frogs, salamanders, snakes, turtles, and crocodiles, thrived. Sharks and rays swam through the oceans alongside enormous plesiosaurs and mosasaurs.

But the stars of the Cretaceous Period were the dinosaurs. Gigantic sauropods lumbered across the land in herds. Birdlike dinosaurs lived in great numbers over most of the globe. Massive horned dinosaurs such as Triceratops lumbered on land. Terrifying meat eaters such as Spinosaurus and Tyrannosaurus rex sat at the top of the food chain.

About 65 million years ago, an asteroid or comet about the size of a small city streaked out of the sky. It struck the Yucatan Peninsula of Mexico.

The explosion it caused was 2 million times stronger than the most powerful human-made bomb. Debris from the explosion flew into the atmosphere and landed, still burning, causing fires across the globe. Earthquakes, volcanic eruptions, and monstrous waves called tsunamis rippled out from the crash site. The smoke and debris in the air blocked out sunlight for years, starving plants of the energy they needed. Plants died, and the Earth grew very cold.

The crater left behind by the explosion has been called the Chicxulub crater after the town that now lies near its center. Scientists are not certain if the Chicxulub collision was the only event that caused more than half of the planet's species to go extinct. It may have been one in a series of collisions that, along with the eruption of many volcanoes, brought an end to the Cretaceous Period.

TIMELINE

252 million years ago••••••••••••••••••••••••••••••••••••••

Paleozoic Era
time of ancient life

Mesozoic Era
time of dinosaurs

251 •••••••••••••200
million years ago   million years ago
TRIASSIC PERIOD

200•••••••••••••••••••••••146
million years ago   million years ago
JURASSIC PERIOD

252 MILLION YEARS AGO
A mass extinction marks
the end of the Paleozoic
Era, sparking a rapid
change in animal and
plant life. The Mesozoic Era
begins, with the first of its
three periods, the Triassic.
The age of reptiles begins.

**210-200
MILLION
YEARS AGO**
Triassic Period
ends, and
Jurassic begins.

**180 MILLION
YEARS AGO**
The Atlantic
Ocean and
Indian Ocean
form as the
supercontinent
Pangaea
breaks apart.

**190 MILLION
YEARS AGO**
The first mammals
appear on Earth.

230-220 MILLION YEARS AGO
The first dinosaurs appear.

**145 MILLION
YEARS AGO**
Jurassic Period
ends, and
Cretaceous begins.

·· 65 million years ago

Cenozoic Era
time of mammals

145 ·· 65
million years ago   million years ago

CRETACEOUS PERIOD

**100-66 MILLION
YEARS AGO
Late Cretaceous**
T. rex reigns.

**65 MILLION
YEARS AGO**
Chicxulub Asteroid
impacts Mexico.
Dinosaurs go extinct.
Cretaceous Period
ends. Cenozoic Era
begins with the
Paleogene Period.
Earth recovers,
temperatures
warm, and modern
mammals appear.

**146-100 MILLION
YEARS AGO
Early Cretaceous**
First flowering plants
evolve, such as magnolia
and ficus. Some groups
of modern insects
appear, including bees,
wasps, beetles, and ants.

23 MILLION YEARS AGO
Neogene Period of the
Cenozoic Era begins.
Grass spreads. New
species of mammals and
other animals evolve.

OTHER PATHS TO EXPLORE

>>> In this book, you time travel to the Cretaceous Period with a friend or two. But what if you were alone? What skills do you have that would be useful? What would be your biggest challenges? Do you think you could survive?

>>> The characters in this story accidentally travel back in time. But what if you traveled back to the Cretaceous Period on purpose? What tools would you bring? What would your goal be?

>>> What if Cretaceous Period dinosaurs could time travel to the present day? What kinds of trouble might they cause for humans? How do you think people could best handle the situation?

READ MORE

Alonso, Juan Carlos. *The Early Cretaceous*. Lake
    Forest, CA: Walter Foster Jr., an imprint of Quarto
    Publishing Group USA Inc., 2017.

Doeden, Matt. *Could You Survive the Jurassic Period?:
    An Interactive Prehistoric Adventure*. North Mankato,
    MN: Capstone, 2019.

Mason, Paul. *Dinosaur Hunters in the Forest*.
    Minneapolis: Hungry Tomato, 2018.

INTERNET SITES

American Museum of Natural History: Dinosaurs
www.amnh.org/dinosaurs

*How Do Paleontologists Reconstruct Environments From
the Ancient Past?*
www.si.edu/object/yt_agJ8_D3JLNg

National Geographic: Cretaceous Period
www.nationalgeographic.com/science/prehistoric-world/
cretaceous/

GLOSSARY

canopy (KA-nuh-pee)—the middle layer of the rain forest where the greenery is thick and there is little sunlight

diorama (dy-uh-RA-muh)—a three-dimensional replication of a scene, often a miniature version

extinct (ik-STINGKT)—no longer living; an extinct animal is one that has died out, with no more of its kind

forage (FOR-ij)—searching, especially for food

gore (GORE)—to pierce with horns

lagoon (luh-GOON)—a shallow area of water between the coast and a coral reef that's offshore

predator (PRED-uh-tur)—an animal that hunts other animals for food

prehistoric (pree-hi-STOR-ik)—from a time before history was recorded

ray (RAY)—a type of fish with a flat body, winglike fins, and a whiplike tail

sauropod (SORE-oh-pod)—a member of a group of closely related dinosaurs with long necks, thick bodies, and long tails

terrarium (tuh-RER-ee-uhm)—a glass or plastic container used for raising land animals; can also be used as a display case

BIBLIOGRAPHY

"Cretaceous Period." National Geographic.com. www.nationalgeographic.com/science/prehistoric-world/cretaceous/>, Accessed March 20, 2019.

Dixon, Dougal. *The Complete Illustrated Encyclopedia of Dinosaurs & Prehistoric Creatures.* Leicester, UK: Southwater, 2014.

"Early Cretaceous Period," HowStuffWorks.com. animals.howstuffworks.com/dinosaurs/early-cretaceous-period.htm, Accessed March 19, 2019.

Everhart, Mike. *Sea Monsters: Prehistoric Creatures of the Deep.* Washington, D.C.: National Geographic Society, 2007.

"Late Cretaceous Period," HowStuffWorks.com. animals.howstuffworks.com/dinosaurs/late-cretaceous-period.htm, Accessed March 19, 2019.

Poinar, George, Jr. and Roberta Poinar. *What Bugged the Dinosaurs? Insects, Disease, and Death in the Cretaceous.* Princeton, NJ: Princeton University Press, 2008.

INDEX

INDEX

BIBLIOGRAPHY

"Cretaceous Period." National Geographic.com. www.nationalgeographic.com/science/prehistoric-world/cretaceous/>, Accessed March 20, 2019.

Dixon, Dougal. *The Complete Illustrated Encyclopedia of Dinosaurs & Prehistoric Creatures.* Leicester, UK: Southwater, 2014.

"Early Cretaceous Period," HowStuffWorks.com. animals.howstuffworks.com/dinosaurs/early-cretaceous-period.htm, Accessed March 19, 2019.

Everhart, Mike. *Sea Monsters: Prehistoric Creatures of the Deep.* Washington, D.C.: National Geographic Society, 2007.

"Late Cretaceous Period," HowStuffWorks.com. animals.howstuffworks.com/dinosaurs/late-cretaceous-period.htm, Accessed March 19, 2019.

Poinar, George, Jr. and Roberta Poinar. *What Bugged the Dinosaurs? Insects, Disease, and Death in the Cretaceous.* Princeton, NJ: Princeton University Press, 2008.